The CATARACT of LODORE

A poem by Robert Southey *Illustrated by* MORDICAI GERSTEIN

DIAL BOOKS FOR YOUNG READERS 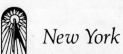 *New York*

For my uncle,
Philip Chornow,
with love M.G.

Published by Dial Books for Young Readers
A Division of Penguin Books USA Inc.
375 Hudson Street
New York, New York 10014

Copyright © 1991 by Mordicai Gerstein
Typography by Mara Nussbaum
Printed in the U.S.A.
First Edition
1 3 5 7 9 10 8 6 4 2

Library of Congress Cataloging in Publication Data
Southey, Robert, 1774–1843.
The cataract of Lodore: a poem / by Robert Southey
illustrated by Mordicai Gerstein. — 1st ed.
p.   cm.
Summary: A poetic description of a famous English
waterfall by the nineteenth-century writer who served as
England's poet laureate for thirty years.
ISBN 0-8037-1025-9. — ISBN 0-8037-1026-7 (library)
1. Waterfalls — Juvenile poetry. 2. Children's poetry, English.
[1. Waterfalls — Poetry. 2. English poetry.]
I. Gerstein, Mordicai, ill. II. Title.
PR5464.C38 1991 821'.7 — dc20 90-44034 CIP AC

——————————————— GLOSSARY ———————————————

brake · *rough or marshy land*
cataract · *a waterfall*
cleave · *to divide, split; also, to stick to or adhere closely*
darkling · *in the dark*
eddying · *moving in a circle; a small whirlpool*
fell · *a high barren field or moor*
gill · *narrow stream or rivulet*
glade · *an open space surrounded by woods*

guggling · *gurgling*
purling · *making a gentle murmur*
rills · *very small brooks*
riving · *tearing apart, dividing, shattering*
smiting · *striking, hitting*
tarn · *mountain lake or pool*
Lodore · *a small waterfall in the Lake District of England*

The ancient Greeks used wreaths
of sacred laurel to crown
their finest artists, athletes, and poets,
who were then called Laureates.
In 1813, Robert Southey,
who called himself "Robert the Rhymer,"
was made Poet Laureate
of England.

"How does the Water
Come down at Lodore?"
My little boy asked me
Thus, once on a time;
And moreover he tasked me
To tell him in rhyme.

Anon at the word,
There first came one daughter
And then came another,
To second and third
The request of their brother,
And to hear how the Water
Comes down at Lodore,
With its rush and its roar,
As many a time
They had seen it before.

So I told them in rhyme,
For of rhymes I had store;
And 'twas in my vocation
For their recreation
That I should sing;
Because I was Laureate
To them and the King.

From its sources which well
In the Tarn on the fell;
From its fountains
In the mountains,
Its rills and its gills;

Through moss and through brake,
It runs and it creeps
For awhile, till it sleeps
In its own little lake.

And thence at departing,
Awakening and starting,
It runs through the reeds
And away it proceeds,
Through meadow and glade,
In sun and in shade,

And through the wood-shelter,
Among crags in its flurry,
Helter-skelter,
Hurry-scurry.

Here it comes sparkling,
And there it lies darkling;
Now smoking and frothing
Its tumult and wrath in,

Till in this rapid race
On which it is bent,
It reaches the place
Of its steep descent.

The Cataract strong
Then plunges along,
Striking and raging
As if a war waging
Its caverns and rocks among:

Rising and leaping,
Sinking and creeping,
Selling and sweeping,
Showering and springing,
Flying and flinging,

Writhing and ringing,

Eddying and whisking,

Spouting and frisking,

Turning and twisting,

Around and around

With endless rebound!

Smiting and fighting,

A sight to delight in;

Confounding, astounding,

Dizzying and deafening the ear with its sound.

Collecting, projecting,
Receding and speeding,

And shocking and rocking,
And darting and parting,
And threading and spreading,

And whizzing and hissing,
And dripping and skipping,

And hitting and splitting,
And shining and twining,
And rattling and battling,

And shaking and quaking,
And pouring and roaring,
And waving and raving,
And tossing and crossing,
And flowing and going,

And running and stunning,
And foaming and roaming,
And dinning and spinning,
And dropping and hopping,
And working and jerking,

And guggling and struggling,

And heaving and cleaving,

And moaning and groaning;

And glittering and frittering,

And gathering and feathering,

And whitening and brightening,

And quivering and shivering,

And hurrying and scurrying,

And thundering and floundering;

Dividing and gliding and sliding,
And falling and brawling and sprawling,
And driving and riving and striving,
And sprinkling and twinkling and wrinkling,

And sounding and bounding and rounding,
And bubbling and troubling and doubling,
And grumbling and rumbling and tumbling,
And clattering and battering and shattering;

Retreating and beating and meeting and sheeting,
Delaying and straying and playing and spraying,
Advancing and prancing and glancing and dancing,
Recoiling, turmoiling and toiling and boiling,

And gleaming and streaming and steaming and beaming,
And rushing and flushing and brushing and gushing,
And flapping and rapping and clapping and slapping,
And curling and whirling and purling and twirling,

And thumping and plumping

and bumping and jumping,

And dashing and flashing

and splashing and clashing;

And so never ending,

but always descending,

Sounds and motions for

ever and ever are blending,

All at once and all o'er,

with a mighty uproar,

And this way

the Water

comes down…

at Lodore.